Pocahontas
the Peacemaker

First published in 2007 by
Franklin Watts
338 Euston Road
London
NW1 3BH

Franklin Watts Australia
Level 17/207 Kent Street
Sydney
NSW 2000

A CIP catalogue record for this book is available
from the British Library.

ISBN 978 0 7496 7080 1 (hbk)
ISBN 978 0 7496 7411 3 (pbk)

Series Editor: Melanie Palmer
Series Advisor: Dr Barrie Wade
Series Designer: Peter Scoulding

Printed in China

Franklin Watts is a division of
Hachette Children's Books.

For Bonnie Jo Hunt,
Oliver, Helena and Amelia – H.R.

Pocahontas
the Peacemaker

by Hilary Robinson and Masumi Furukawa

W

FRANKLIN WATTS
LONDON•SYDNEY

About this book

Some of the characters in this book are made up, but the subject is based on real events in history. Pocahontas (1595–1617) was born in a village in Virginia, North America. She was the daughter of Chief Powhaten, leader of the village. When some English people arrived, they built a town called Jamestown. It was named after the English King, James I. Pocahontas visited the English people and became friends with Captain John Smith. She helped bring peace between the English and her people by encouraging the trade of food, clothing and tools. She later married an Englishman, John Rolfe. She lived in England until 1617, when she died from illness.

The whole village celebrated when
a beautiful princess was born.
"We will call her Pocahontas,"
said her father, Chief Powhaten.

5

As she grew up, Pocahontas
helped the villagers with their jobs.
She made clay pots to carry water.

She watched the men build canoes.

When the hunters returned, she
gathered firewood to cook fish
and buffalo meat.

For many years, everyone lived
peacefully. They farmed the
land and shared big meals.

Life was quiet until ... the strangers arrived! They had sailed far across the sea, from a land called England.

The Chief was angry and shouted: "These people want to take our land. We won't let them stay!"

He sent his men to spy on the English and capture their leader, Captain James Smith.

Captain Smith was caught
and taken to Chief Powhaten.
"We come in peace. We want to
help you," promised the Captain.

"No," roared the Chief.

"You want to take our land,
then kill us with your guns!"

Captain Smith was forced to kneel down. The Chief's men raised their weapons. Pocahontas couldn't just watch anymore ...

14

She threw herself in front of
the Captain and begged:
"Stop! Father, he can help us!"
She began to cry.

The Chief was shocked. He dropped his spear. He had never seen Pocahontas look so upset.

"Please, Father, take pity!" she said.

The Chief stopped feeling angry.

"If my daughter wants the Captain

to live ... let him live," he said.

But life was not easy for the English. The local people did not like them living so close by.

Pocahontas knew she would have to work hard to keep the peace. "Perhaps we could all help each other," she thought.

The Chief still got angry at times.
He was ready to attack if the
English came near his village.

B-8₽₣d0g

Pocahontas even risked her own life to meet the English, to warn them about her father.

Soon the English began to starve.
They did not know how to farm
the land and grow food.

Pocahontas wanted to help. She
crept secretly through the forest,
carrying food to Captain Smith.

The English were grateful and
called Pocahontas their angel.

They swapped their tools for
fresh food and new clothes.

When Pocahontas returned home,
she went to see her father, saying:
"Look, they have brought us
presents from England."

The Chief was pleased and took the English tools – but he did not know how to use them!

Pochaontas laughed at the Chief. Then she had an idea. "Let's ask the English to show us how to use their tools."

The Chief did not want to ask for help. Then Pocahontas told him how bad the English were at farming. "We could help each other," she said.

So the English showed the
villagers how to use the tools.
In return, the villagers helped
them farm the land.

Years later, Captain Smith returned
to England. He told Queen Anne,
wife of King James I, all about
Pocahontas the peacemaker.

Hopscotch has been specially designed to fit the requirements of the National Literacy Strategy. It offers real books by top authors and illustrators for children developing their reading skills. There are 49 Hopscotch stories to choose from:

Marvin, the Blue Pig
ISBN 978 0 7496 4619 6

Plip and Plop
ISBN 978 0 7496 4620 2

The Queen's Dragon
ISBN 978 0 7496 4618 9

Flora McQuack
ISBN 978 0 7496 4621 9

Willie the Whale
ISBN 978 0 7496 4623 3

Naughty Nancy
ISBN 978 0 7496 4622 6

Run!
ISBN 978 0 7496 4705 6

The Playground Snake
ISBN 978 0 7496 4706 3

"Sausages!"
ISBN 978 0 7496 4707 0

The Truth about Hansel and Gretel
ISBN 978 0 7496 4708 7

Pippin's Big Jump
ISBN 978 0 7496 4710 0

Whose Birthday Is It?
ISBN 978 0 7496 4709 4

The Princess and the Frog
ISBN 978 0 7496 5129 9

Flynn Flies High
ISBN 978 0 7496 5130 5

Clever Cat
ISBN 978 0 7496 5131 2

Moo!
ISBN 978 0 7496 5332 3

Izzie's Idea
ISBN 978 0 7496 5334 7

Roly-poly Rice Ball
ISBN 978 0 7496 5333 0

I Can't Stand It!
ISBN 978 0 7496 5765 9

Cockerel's Big Egg
ISBN 978 0 7496 5767 3

How to Teach a Dragon Manners
ISBN 978 0 7496 5873 1

The Truth about those Billy Goats
ISBN 978 0 7496 5766 6

Marlowe's Mum and the Tree House
ISBN 978 0 7496 5874 8

Bear in Town
ISBN 978 0 7496 5875 5

The Best Den Ever
ISBN 978 0 7496 5876 2

ADVENTURE STORIES

Aladdin and the Lamp
ISBN 978 0 7496 6692 7

Blackbeard the Pirate
ISBN 978 0 7496 6690 3

George and the Dragon
ISBN 978 0 7496 6691 0

Jack the Giant-Killer
ISBN 978 0 7496 6693 4

TALES OF KING ARTHUR

1. The Sword in the Stone
ISBN 978 0 7496 6694 1

2. Arthur the King
ISBN 978 0 7496 6695 8

3. The Round Table
ISBN 978 0 7496 6697 2

4. Sir Lancelot and the Ice Castle
ISBN 978 0 7496 6698 9

TALES OF ROBIN HOOD

Robin and the Knight
ISBN 978 0 7496 6699 6

Robin and the Monk
ISBN 978 0 7496 6700 9

Robin and the Friar
ISBN 978 0 7496 6702 3

Robin and the Silver Arrow
ISBN 978 0 7496 6703 0

FAIRY TALES

The Emperor's New Clothes
ISBN 978 0 7496 7077 1 *
ISBN 978 0 7496 7421 2

Cinderella
ISBN 978 0 7496 7073 3 *
ISBN 978 0 7496 7417 5

Snow White
ISBN 978 0 7496 7074 0 *
ISBN 978 0 7496 7418 2

Jack and the Beanstalk
ISBN 978 0 7496 7078 8 *
ISBN 978 0 7496 7422 9

The Three Billy Goats Gruff
ISBN 978 0 7496 7076 4 *
ISBN 978 0 7496 7420 5

The Pied Piper of Hamelin
ISBN 978 0 7496 7075 7 *
ISBN 978 0 7496 7419 9

HISTORIES

Toby and the Great Fire of London
ISBN 978 0 7496 7079 5 *
ISBN 978 0 7496 7410 6

Pocahontas the Peacemaker
ISBN 978 0 7496 7080 1 *
ISBN 978 0 7496 7411 3

Grandma's Seaside Bloomers
ISBN 978 0 7496 7081 8 *
ISBN 978 0 7496 7412 0

Hoorah for Mary Seacole
ISBN 978 0 7496 7082 5 *
ISBN 978 0 7496 7413 7

Remember the 5th of November
ISBN 978 0 7496 7083 2 *
ISBN 978 0 7496 7414 4

Tutankhamun and the Golden Chariot
ISBN 978 0 7496 7084 9 *
ISBN 978 0 7496 7415 1

* hardback